HarperCollins®, ®, HarperFestival®, and Festival Readers™
are trademarks of HarperCollins Publishers Inc.
Harold and the Purple Crayon: Animals, Animals, Animals!
Text copyright © 2002 by Adelaide Productions, Inc.
Illustrations copyright © 2002 by Adelaide Productions, Inc.
Printed in the U.S.A. All rights reserved.
Library of Congress catalog card number: 2001097083
www.harperchildrens.com

1 2 3 4 5 6 7 8 9 10
❖
First Edition

HAROLD and the PURPLE CRAYON™

Animals, Animals, Animals!

Adaptation by Liza Baker
Based on a teleplay by Don Gillies
Illustrations by Andy Chiang,
Jose Lopez, and Kevin Murawski

HarperFestival®
A Division of HarperCollinsPublishers

Harold couldn't sleep,

so he took out his stuffed animals.

Harold thought about

how much fun animals have.

What animal would I like to be?

he wondered.

Harold wanted to find out
more about animals.

He picked up his purple crayon
and set off on an adventure.

Harold thought,

I would like to be big and strong.

He took his crayon and drew an elephant.

The elephant dipped its trunk

into a bucket of water.

Then he sprayed water all around.

It looked like fun.

So Harold drew a hose.

But the hose was very wiggly.

Harold accidentally sprayed the elephant.

The elephant got all wet.

Harold tried to apologize,

but the elephant walked away.

I would like to take long trips,

thought Harold.

So he drew a camel.

Then Harold drew a large backpack
full of food and water.
Together, Harold and the camel
set off through the desert.

As Harold walked,

the backpack felt very heavy.

Harold was tired.

The sun was hot.

He drew a lake and a palm tree.

As Harold rested,

a herd of cheetahs ran by.

I would like to move really fast,

thought Harold.

Harold drew a pair of roller skates
and raced after the cheetahs.

Racing with the cheetahs was fun,

but soon Harold was hot again.

He wanted to go somewhere cool.

Harold took his crayon

and drew a line up to the sky.

He found himself on

top of a snow-covered hill.

Harold met a group of penguins.
They were sliding one by one on
their bellies down the slope.

I would like to slide down a snowy hill, thought Harold.

So he drew a sled.

Many penguins jumped on with Harold.

Soon the sled was full of penguins.

The sled sped down the hill.

With a crash, Harold and the
penguins landed in the snow.

Harold was covered with snow.

He was cold.

He drew a big sun in the sky.

Harold was warm again.

He drew a jungle.

Monkeys played on vines.

I would like to swing, thought Harold.

He reached up and grabbed a vine.

Soon he was swinging back and forth

just like the monkeys.

Living the life of the animals

had been fun.

But Harold liked being himself best.

Harold took his purple crayon and
drew his bedroom window.

Back in his room,

Harold pulled up his covers.

As he hugged Lilac in his arms,

his purple crayon dropped to the floor,

and Harold dropped off to sleep.

A NOTE TO PARENTS

Welcome to the world of Festival Readers! These inviting, high-interest readers were created to help develop and nurture a love of reading as children enjoy adventures about their favorite characters.

Reading is an increasingly important skill in society, and the foundation you lay for your child in the early years plays a key role in his or her future reading success. As your child's "first teacher," your contribution is vital. Here are some hints you may find helpful:

- Find a comfortable setting in which to read together. You might create a "reading corner" in your child's room or any quiet place.
- Read the book together again and again to build reading fluency.
- Look at the pictures together on each page and discuss what is happening and why. Ask your child to predict what will happen on the next page, or speculate aloud as you read.

We hope that you and your child enjoy the pleasure this story brings, and that your child's world will be enriched and expanded by the adventure of reading!

FESTIVAL READERS

HAROLD and the PURPLE CRAYON™

Harold loves animals so much that he decides to find out what it's like to be one. Join Harold and an elephant, a camel, a herd of cheetahs, and a slippery bunch of penguins on this wildlife adventure in his imagination.

Don't miss these other adventures:

HAROLD and the PURPLE CRAYON.
The Birthday Present

HAROLD and the PURPLE CRAYON.
The Giant Garden

HAROLD and the PURPLE CRAYON.
Harold Finds a Friend

HarperFestival®
A Division of HarperCollinsPublishers

Ages 4–7
TM & © 2002 Adelaide Productions, Inc. All Rights Reserved.
Cover © 2002 by Adelaide Productions, Inc.
Cover art by Kevin Murawski
www.harperchildrens.com

US $3.99 / $5.99 CAN
ISBN 0-06-000177-1

0 46594 00399 7

PINK TAG
TALIZE

P9-AMJ-334

A